TINKERMAN

TINKERMAN

AN ORIGINAL STORY

THOMAS C. MAYO

Tinkerman

Copyright © 2020 by Thomas C. Mayo. All rights reserved.

No part of this publication may be reproduced, stored in a retrieval system or transmitted in any way by any means, electronic, mechanical, photocopy, recording or otherwise without the prior permission of the author except as provided by USA copyright law.

This novel is a work of fiction. Names, descriptions, entities, and incidents included in the story are products of the author's imagination. Any resemblance to actual persons, events, and entities is entirely coincidental.

The opinions expressed by the author are not necessarily those of URLink Print and Media.

1603 Capitol Ave., Suite 310 Cheyenne, Wyoming USA 82001
1-888-980-6523 | admin@urlinkpublishing.com

URLink Print and Media is committed to excellence in the publishing industry.

Book design copyright © 2020 by URLink Print and Media. All rights reserved.

Published in the United States of America

Library of Congress Control Number: 2019919908
ISBN 978-1-64753-101-0 (Paperback)
ISBN 978-1-64753-102-7 (Digital)

18.11.19

CONTENTS

Chapter 1: Swimming with Sharks 7
Chapter 2: The Meeting 10
Chapter 3: Mr. Green 13
Chapter 4: Comrades 16
Chapter 5: Silent Screams 20
Chapter 6: Almost There 24
Chapter 7: Home 26
Chapter 8: Family? 27
Chapter 9: Invention 30
Chapter 10: Bada Boom 31
Chapter 11: The Price 34
Chapter 12: Mr. Green Revealed 37
Chapter 13: It's on Now 38
Chapter 14: The Mountain 42
Chapter 15: Good-Byes 45
Chapter 16: The Chase 47
Chapter 17: Small Town Blues 50
Chapter 18: All Aboard 52
Chapter 19: I'm Your Captain 54
Chapter 20: Triangle 55
Chapter 21: Into the Drink 57

CHAPTER 1

Swimming with Sharks

GEORGE AND STEVEN stand behind the door for introductions. "Are you nervous?" he says to his friend as he does the Groucho eyebrows shake. But Steven just shakes it off, saying, "We've got this right? I mean this thing has helped everyone we've ever used it on and that's why I'm endorsing you, buddy!" as he pats him on the shoulder. Just then, a stagehand opens the door and tells them the camera's rolling as they head toward the sharks. It's now eight o'clock at night, and they've been in town for two days, prepping for this very moment. "Good evening, Sharks! I'm Steven and this is George, and we're here to present the, ahhh, table to you in hopes of getting 200,000 dollars for 2 percent of the business. And we invite you to lay on it and see if it doesn't make you feel 100 percent better! I'm a chiropractor and I use it in my business, and we are now renting time slots on it at my office, and it's nonstop, all day, every day, at fifteen-minute intervals each. We're booked for months in advance."

The first one to chime in is Kevin Oleary, a.k.a. Mr. Wonderful. "We don't want to feel better, we want to be richer! What does it do, and how much does it cost to make? And what does it retail for?"

Lori Greiner jumps up from her seat in a form-flattering dress and says, "I want to try it. It's been a while since I've been to the spa and I could use a massage!" She proceeds to sit on the edge, then lies down. George walks over and hits the switch that turns it on. Multiple massagers start humming on her back, and she lets out an

"Ahhh!" She starts to relax immediately and says, "Ooh! This is really kind of nice," as she lifts up off it and starts to head back up to the stage area.

"Wait a second, you're gonna need this." Steven bends down to grab a cheap wooden back scratcher and hands it to her. She immediately reaches behind her head and starts itching feverishly. Mark Cuban jumps in with, "It's ten bucks for the table, but ten thousand for the back scratcher!" And they all start laughing!

Daymond John folds his arms together and gets real serious and says, "Seriously, how much does it cost to make this thing?"

George quickly responds, "350 to 400 dollars."

Again, Daymond says, "And how much is it retail?"

Steven takes this one, "1,200."

Kevin joins the fray. "And how many have you sold?" The two look at each other, then back at the Sharks and yell, "None!" All the sharks are throwing hands up, laughing and acting disgusted and offended.

It is Lori who speaks first. "Then why are you even here?"

George replies, "We were hoping you'd be the first!"

Now they were really laughing! The host intervenes and says, "Lori?"

"Well," she explains, "it would be hard for me to move on QVC or any of my stores for that matter, and for that reason, I am out. It did feel good though."

Next is Kevin. "That thing would just put me to sleep ... like your presentation did. I'm out!"

Daymond says, "If you can find a way to make it cheaper, and throw in a free back scratcher. But till then, I'm out."

And that just left Mark Cuban. "You seem to be on to something here. Why does it itch so bad after using it?"

Steven looks to George, who then replies, "After the muscles have been stimulated that have not worked in a while, they come alive and start to itch. It's a good thing."

Mark is almost interested. "Do you have a patent on it? And what makes it different from all the other massagers out there?"

Steven takes this one. "It's the placement. I have others at my practice that are similar, but none have the coverage that this one does." He seems nervous, almost desperate, like he knows the deal is almost lost. "If you can start marketing better, and you start to move it, let me know. I'm out. Do you have any other inventions besides this one?"

George says, "Yes, yes, I'm working on a magnetic engine that takes no fuel or electricity, but I'm having some friction problems from the rotation of the gears around the axle."

Kevin yells over, "Now that we'd be interested in."

They head out to the hall where they are greeted by a cameraman for an after-shark commentary.

Steven speaks first. "Ah, we took the sharks' suggestions, and we will continue to use it as is for the ones who do use it … love it."

And that was it. They catch a cab with the table folded in half and head off to the airport. Steven bumps George as they walk off the plane to catch separate cabs to go home. "You want to go for drinks later?"

George smiles. "Yeah, I could use one."

CHAPTER 2

The Meeting

TINKER ALWAYS DAYDREAMED as a child. He understood the nature of things early, how the universe was made up of various gasses, plasma, and, yes, magnetism. And how, if anything in the rotation of the earth moved too far in either direction, life as we know it would cease to exist. A perfect alignment was necessary for energy to thrive and magnetism was universal. When two magnetic objects are attracted to each other, alignment for energy is the distance between them. Too far, they stop moving, too close, they connect and movement stops.

He was constantly reminded of magnetism at the hospital during his wife Mary's cancer treatments. Doors opened only to be held by magnets until released. A giant magnet took scans of her, etc., etc. He had actually met her in high school. Being a small town, everyone knew everyone else's business, but she had just moved there and before class had begun, she was watching him walk by with one shoe untied. George was looking skyward and twirling his hand in the air as if calculating some unknown equation on a mental chalkboard in his mind. She'd jumped up from the stairs she was sitting on and ran in front of him, putting both hands on his chest to stop him. "Excuse me!" she boldly stated. "You are about to walk into a sign!"

He stopped. As their eyes met, he had lost all concentration and thought. "W-What?" he muttered.

"And your shoe's untied." She bent down on one knee to tie it for him and he noticed the sign pole in front of him. As he looked at the top of her hair in front of his groin area, he realized for the first time in his life his body could be attracted to this girl. When she finished, she popped back up, giving him an intoxicating whiff of her perfume, and he felt an undeniable wanting for her.

"Now you try and be more careful, you just never know what you'll bump into." With a foxy wink, she walked off, leaving him with his jaw wide open and the beginning of what will be many hard-ons for Mary.

This is what he was thinking of as he arrived at the town hall for a meeting after the show that changed his life. The police were at his house anyway once he had reported the break-in which left his house devastated. After they took his information, he was asked politely to let them escort him. They said the mayor called the meeting after the arrival of a number of men, all claiming to be from the power companies. He was led down an aisle between numerous folding tables to a stage with stairs leading to it. In the middle of the stage was a podium with a table on the right where four men he had never seen sat, acting restless. On the other side of the podium were the mayor, the chief of police, and two town council members.

George was directed to a metal chair next to the podium, where he sat and looked out upon an obviously nervous audience. He had a small engine-and- appliance repair business that, coupled with the dwindling social security benefits and life insurance policy from his wife's death, managed to keep him able to pay a mortgage and raise two boys. He knew these people well. He had fixed things for them on many occasions through the years, and now here they were in the middle of the night to help decide the fate of this town concerning a problem that, up until a short time ago, didn't exist. George changed tires, fixed cars, computers, you name it. He had magnetic signs made for his truck which read "All You Need Is Tinker!"

The townsfolk all got together on holidays, picnics, etc. It's a small, little Connecticut town called Nightwood, with a population of about ten thousand or so. They were very domesticated, church-going, hardworking, somewhat happy.

The first to speak was Mayor Clayton Wayburn. A stout fellow with a big red tie, always pushing some town agenda. "People of Nightwood!" He tries to quiet numerous conversations while yelling and tapping a gavel. "This affects all of us!"

The room quiets down. "First of all, I'm sorry to drag you all down here, but let's hear what these men have to say." With that, he gestured with his hand to the first suited man, who stood up and walked to the podium. "Good people of Nightwood, I am Mr. Jefferson from homeland security in Washington, and this man has a device that could upset all life as we know it!"

George jumped to his feet. "Now wait just a minute!" he shouted. Two large men rushed from the table and pushed him back down on the seat and held his shoulders to make sure he wouldn't move.

"If anyone in this town is holding this device for George Tinker, they will be subject to search and seizure of property and arrested!"

The room erupted! The two men grabbed George under the arms to forcibly remove him out a side door to a parking lot. He could hear shouts of "Just let him go!" and "Give it to them, George!" in the distance.

CHAPTER 3

Mr. Green

OUTSIDE, A LONG black limousine with dark windows and the door already opened, waited for George. The two men gently pushed him in and shut the door. "Hello, George … or should I call you Tinker?" Inside was a man with a soft, soothing voice who seemed to be the one pulling the strings. He was wearing a black suit and a long black trench coat.

"What the fuck is happening?"

A smile crossed the man's face as he leaned over to look directly in George's eyes and poke a finger against his chest.

"You are, George." he states.

"What is all this? Please let me go!"

The man sat back and faced forward. "All this? You did this. You went on national TV and mentioned a device which needed no fuel. Do you realize the panic you have caused my world?" As he looked over, he lifted his dark glasses to reveal sinister-looking eyes. George felt a little uneasy when he saw them and said, "Who the fuck are you?"

But he was still not afraid. "I am the future, the past, the present. I am Mr. Green to you because I am offering you twenty million dollars for your device or take it from you by force. But we are both intelligent men and everyone has a price. I have turned your whole town against you and, with enough media spin, soon the whole country as well. You got lucky and stumbled upon something which you have no idea how to apply. But I do, and I can help you."

George thinks to himself, *This guy is smooth.* He says softly, "And if I refuse?"

There was a slight chuckle from Mr. Green. "Refusal would not be the best strategy at this point, George. By the way, we've gone through all of your possessions, inventions, refrigerator, we can't seem to find it. Does it even exist?"

This man got under his skin like no other in his lifetime. He could feel the anger seeping in like it was shot into his veins. "Mr. Green ... I have known men like you before, using fear to manipulate, and all your weapons of intimidation to control the outcome of a particular event. You treat people like rats in a maze. We hold no importance to you whatsoever, except amusement. You offer twenty million for what is worth billions if it works, but you don't want it to work because if it does, you'll no longer need that gas engine Henry Ford invented in, umm ... 1902? How can you topple governments and control tyrants if you don't control any and all power? What people don't know is when they're running from a monster in their dreams, that monster is you." He points at Mr. Green forcefully. Behind Tinker, the door swings open, and the same large man that had thrown him in there now grabbed a handful of shirt from his shoulder area and pulled him from the car.

"You have forty-eight hours to produce the magnetic engine. I suggest you use it wisely," was what George heard as he hit the ground face first. He got up and started brushing himself off as he watched the limo and two black SUVs slip away into the dark night. "You'll never get it," he murmured to himself as an arm slipped around his throat, clamping him into a headlock. He struggled to maintain balance, fighting for air, until the cloth was shoved on and covered his mouth and nose. Chloroform.

George looked to the sky as the twinkle of stars lead him to an ever- growing blackness. He dreamed of planets and quasars, nebulas, a black hole sucking in light from a dying star ... and then his groggy eyes opened to a half-naked woman whose curvy silhouette stood in front of the balcony sunlight.

"W-wh-who are you?" he stuttered out, throat still raspy from chloroform.

"I am your gift, my American friend. Welcome to Russia!"

CHAPTER 4

Comrades

SHE CRAWLED OVER him, leaned in to kiss him, and he turned away before she can.

"Am I not pretty?" She asked with her pouty, blinking eyes.

"Yes ... yes, you are very pretty."

She could tell he was being honest. "Are you gay? Because we could make some arrangements?"

He gave her a startled look. "No, I'm not gay, I still love my wife!"

She climbed off him. "Oh, please, we did our research, she's been dead for ten years." Her words sharply reminded him of how long it's been.

"She's not dead ... we ... we don't really die, but our essence takes a different form ... becomes something else." He was thinking of the universe again, gasses, plasma, magnetism, all having purpose. Death having meaning. She realized she had never known a man such as this her whole life, and her charms would do no good here. As she headed back toward the balcony, she looked up to the corner of the ceiling and signaled a camera that had gone unnoticed till now. Suddenly, a wall started opening, then another. *This was all staged,* George thought to himself.

Behind the walls was an elaborate information center with multiple screens showing everything from the Middle East, to America.

"Mr. Tinka ... [in heavy Russian accent] ... It looks like you are in a great deal of trouble, da?" A tall, older man emerges from the shadows in uniform with a scar on his left cheek. Definitely a knife or a shank of some kind, but George didn't want to know.

"We do not want a race with America for your device. In fact, I'm sure you have already given your invention to them, which is why my men grabbed you after leaving Mr. Green's car."

This Russian man paced back and forth, occasionally putting his hands behind his back while walking. George was still lying in the bed, half sitting up.

"I am Vladimir Koskov, head of Russian military. We are going to give you a warehouse full of everything you need to build another one. We understand the importance of an engine that runs without fuel, and we can bring in other defectors that will help you to live here and work quite comfortably." He stopped pacing.

George stood up to walk over and look him directly in the eyes. "I am not a defector, I am here against my will, and no one has received my engine yet because as I stated on the show earlier, I'm having friction problems. Now, please, let me go!"

Vladimir walked over, leaned in, and said, "Are you afraid to die, Mr. Tinka?"

Just then, a soldier walked in, saluted, and said, "Urgent call from the US. A Mr. Green." Vladimir walked away and began shouting on the phone. Then he left the room, slamming the door, and was replaced by two soldiers who flanked each side of him and asked him to come with them. They slipped a cloth bag over his head, which stopped him from seeing, but it felt like forever as they walked down long corridors, through doors, downstairs into a waiting vehicle.

After fifteen minutes or so, they lifted the bag and pulled up in front of the American embassy. "Enjoy your stay in Russia." And they let him out and sped off. George could see the marines just beyond the gate and was just about to enter when he heard, "Pssst!"

He looked over to the right and, dressed differently, was the girl from the balcony.

"Oh, hey, um … I don't even know your name." She ran to his side and with both hands, started pulling on his right arm toward her. "It's Tatiana, but that's not important right now. You must come with me. I told my grandmother about you, and she wants to meet you!"

He looked at her like she was crazy and started to head back toward the embassy. "I'm sure she's really nice, but I've got to—"

She cut him off. "No! You don't understand! She's a psychic. I'm a … we … we're Gypsies from Romania, and my grandmother is famous all over Russia for predicting events that come true! Give me five minutes, and I'll bring you right back, I promise."

They walked through poor neighborhoods to a large apartment complex that had about ten floors. She stated that the elevator never works, but luckily, they lived on the fourth floor. After stepping into the dimly lit hallway, they felt their way to the second door, and she pulled out a keychain and opened three locks. Down the hall were the sounds of people screaming at each other in Russian, behind one door was the sound of a baby crying, there was music behind another, and a loud television from yet another.

They stepped inside, and it was amazingly quiet. Through the kitchen and past a beaded doorway was an old, leathery-faced woman wearing a scarf on her head and what seemed to be a full-length flowered dress (she most likely made it herself, and it was obviously her favorite.) with thick socks and work boots. Her eyes looked nearly shut. George thought she might be sleeping, but then he realized that was just how they were. She seemed like she'd seen much labor throughout her life, and she appeared extremely weather beaten. She slowly rocked away in an old, creaky, rocking chair. There was just a radio that was not turned on and a sofa. George walked up, bent halfway down to look her in the face, and then said, "Hello! Nice to meet you!" He started to leave when the old woman unexpectedly grabbed his hand. He suddenly felt a chill down his spine like nothing he'd ever felt before. And he drifted out of consciousness.

He was aware that he was still standing there, but now he was in his mind drifting through space, watching comets speed by … the birth of a star … rings of Saturn, particles of meteors … and in the background was the sound of the old woman rambling in Romanian dialect like she had just found her sole purpose in life. George's hands were again reaching skyward, like he was typing and rearranging planets, and as quickly as it started, it stopped. His legs became wobbly, and he moved to sit down on the ragged sofa next to the old woman's chair that had been covered with sheets to hide the wear and the runs in the fabric. "What just happened?"

Tatiana's eyes were wide with surprise. "Grandmother said you are star born and hold the key to space travel!" She was slightly shouting.

"You mean stubborn," he said with a slight smirk. He sensed the old woman may have seen what he saw and that set her off. She was now rocking quickly and looking into nothing while muttering, moving her head back and forth.

"I'm going." George rose to his feet.

"I'll walk you back."

He was actually starting to enjoy her company, he mused to himself as she slid her arm inside his. The cool air filled their lungs as their pace quickened. She, too, must have the gift as well, for she sensed that they are in danger, and yet she enjoyed the company of a man who was not interested in abusing or using her in some way. She looked up at him and smiled. "You know, your wife was really a lucky wo—"

A fast zip, a noise from behind as her chest exploded! She slid down the side of his arm as he tried to cradle her head in his hands. Black blood oozed from her mouth. She has already slipped away. He shook his head in disbelief while tears formed in his eyes. "Tatiana! Tatiana!" He looked at her face and saw his wife's image. "M-M-Mary?" Then *bam!* Blunt object to the back of the head. Darkness engulfed him as he felt the warm blood trickle down his face. This time, when he awakened, the air is hot.

CHAPTER 5

Silent Screams

SPOTLIGHTS SHONE ON him and he started to feel a large headache coming on. Someone dressed him in an orange jumpsuit, and he felt a hand holding his neck. He knew he'd been drugged because he had no strength to fight back. His glasses were slightly scratched, and he looked up to try and see beyond the lights. So hard to focus …

Once he saw the camera and the man wearing a turban shouting into it, he realized where he was. "We will cut off the infidel's head, if ten million dollars is not delivered tomorrow by one p.m."

He was seriously considering Mr. Green's offer at this point, but somehow, he knew this was not the end. Perhaps it was what the old woman said … star born. "What does that even mean?" he asked himself.

More talk in Arabic, and then one of them yelled, "Shhh!" and all went quiet. The spotlight was shut off. Everyone went silent to listen for the noise they thought they heard. Machine guns in the distance confirm their fears. Several bursts indicate a large number of men trying to surround a smaller group. Many men dropped what they were doing and picked up rifles; they started heading toward the battle.

With little light, he saw the shadows scattered across a rock wall, and he knew he was in a cave. The drugs were starting to wear off because he felt less groggy, but he still couldn't rise. A bearded man ran over to him, flipped him on his back, and duct taped his mouth, then whispered, "If you make a fucking sound, American dog, I will gut you like pig." The bearded man then shut the remaining light and disappeared into the blackness. George was extremely uncomfortable with his hands tied, mouth taped, legs wobbly from the drugs, and alone in the dark. He heard precise bursts of small arms fire from a distance. Then closer and closer still … then right outside … three shots … the thud of a body hitting the dirt floor. Whispers all around him … sounds … American! A bright light illuminated his whole face as someone bent down and pulled the tape off. "Are you Tinker?"

He shook his head repeatedly in a furious yes, and then says, "Yes, are you the good guys?"

The man said, "Yes we are, sir." Then he put his finger to his mouth and whispered, "Shh." The man grabbed his shoulder and lifted him up. George was still unsteady, so the man held him up, while he cut the ropes on his wrists which brought instant relief from the cutoff circulation. "Here, put these on." And he put a change of clothes in his hands—black ops fatigues like they all wore. George couldn't get out of the orange jump suit fast enough. It was a little awkward being the only one dressing in the glow of the flashlight, but once he'd finished, it clicked off. A different soldier then put something on his head. "These are NVGs. Night vision goggles. We will be leading you to safety, so use them to stay with us. Keep them on until you are safe. Do you understand?"

Still slightly whispering, he answered, "Y-yes, I get it. But who are you?"

No one made a sound but the one soldier that talked to him first. "Let's just say that's classified, we're special ops with orders from the top to get you back on your way, so please follow us sir." The goggles showed green illumination around everything and he looked to see what his companions looked like, but they were all wearing masks that cover their faces for purposes of sand and stealth. What little did show had black war paint covering it to cut glare. Even though he didn't see them or know them, he felt a certain calmness about them, like they have it all under control. "How did you find me?"

They were still walking. "Eyes in the sky, sir." The soldier said as little as possible. They reached the outside of the caves and started to make their way down a ravine to an open field with huge boulders on the outskirts that they took cover behind. Shots from a distant sniper shattered bits and pieces of the rock in front of them as they tried to pinpoint location. No one fired a shot yet.

Suddenly, George is overwhelmed by his vision of a giant meteorite shower in space and started walking into the field with his hands in the air like he was holding an invisible typewriter and he was story bound!

"What the fuck is he doing?" Yelled one of the soldiers.

"I don't know," yelled another.

"Well, get after him before he gets killed," said the obvious leader of the group. And with that, two men jumped out and assumed flanking positions on both sides of George, who was still in a trance, wandering forward to some unknown destination. And just like that, he came out of it. The twirling beat of a helicopter came out of nowhere and fired a rocket toward the sniper's general direction, then landed in the field.

One of the soldiers grabbed George and says, "Welcome back, sir, are you going to be okay?"

George kind of shrugged, and they all climbed in and assumed a watching position while George took a much-needed rest on the floor and heaved a sigh of relief.

"Do you believe in God, sir?" The question came from behind him. It was the leader of the team. George still couldn't see faces. "W-what?" It caught George a little off guard.

"What I just saw, sir, that sniper had you dead to rights, but you didn't even flinch, like you were possessed or something. So I ask you, do you believe in God?"

A bit of silence, like he was trying to put it into words properly. "I believe man is incapable of fathoming God. From what I know of the universe, man is lucky to live seventy-five to one hundred years while stars and galaxies live on for millions. I know of an energy that controls many things, like the birth of stars. But does that make a nebula God? My wife made me promise to meet her at Heaven's gate before she died, so I'm going to say yes. And from what I've seen, people seem to be more violent these days and one might argue it's because of or a lack of religion. I have felt an energy form … a presence surround me once, when I was eight." George was babbling more to himself than them.

Eight was when it all started. The presence that surrounded him, and then he became aware of things. The sky seemed to touch the earth like a giant invisible finger. From then on, he could hear the hum of a smooth-running engine or the knock of a bad one before anyone else. His adopted parents didn't understand him, which was why he left and changed his name to Tinker. "I'm from a small town in Connecticut, church on Sunday was a way of life till my wife died. How about you guys?"

Only the leader answered, "With us, it's not a question … it's the only answer. We're going to set it down, now, sir. But you are in a safe zone, now. No enemies for dozens of miles." He pointed. "Just over that ridge is a temporary base set up, and they will see you the rest of the way home."

They can see the glow over the ridge.

"You guys aren't coming with me?"

No one even looked his way. "We're needed elsewhere, sir." They lift off and escape into the blackness of night.

CHAPTER 6

Almost There

AFTER A QUICK walk over the hill, he arrived at the base with two sets of guards greeting him and leading him through two sets of gates. He was escorted to a large tent in the center of camp that had all kinds of video screens that monitored the surrounding area. He'd been frisked several times and asked numerous times how he'd gotten military-grade fatigues and ended up at a top secret, remote covert base. He had lost all forms of identification during his ordeal. They placed him in a chair, in front of a cigar-smoking colonel with guards on each side. The colonel bent, puffed into his face, and asked, "Who the fuck are you and why are you here?"

George answered with some slight hesitation. "I am George Tinker from Nightwood, Connecticut, and I just left a helicopter full of men that dropped me over the hill and said I would be safe here. Didn't they tell you I was coming?"

The look of bewilderment on the colonel's face gave George a bit of uneasiness. "We have no birds in the air and all of my men are accounted for, so you'd better have a better story, my friend."

George was adamant about his answer. "But that's not possible, what about a different base or something because it just happened."

The colonel was interrupted by an urgent phone call. "It's a Mr. Green, sir, direct from the Pentagon." The colonel took the phone and after a minute of talking, walked over to hand it to George.

"Hello?"

A familiar voice was on the other end. "Are you done fuckin' around, George, coz we're ready to make a better offer this time. We *want* you to build it so everyone can see it's in the land of the free. What d'ya say, Georgie boy, are we in business?"

The colonel pulled a gun from his holster, cocked it, and put it to George's head. He was really starting to loathe this guy. "Do I have a choice?" *Click!*

A hot shower, a change of clothes, and that afternoon, a convoy of armored personnel carriers arrived to escort him to an airbase where he flew out, never to be seen there again.

CHAPTER 7

Home

*A*HH, HOME SWEET *home,* George thought to himself. It felt good to be here, working on things again, and after the last week, even more so. George didn't even mind the guard in the unmarked car in the driveway outside his door. The garage is full of clutter. Mrs. Lederman's leaf blower from next door needed a new cord. This one was special because of one of his best friends since his wife died, Emma. She was an eight-year-old girl whose parents were put in prison after numerous failed attempts at quitting drugs. Their drug addiction caused a small crime spree to which there was only one end. Her grandmother had custody of her. There were various lawn mowers, snow blowers, even a dirt bike took up the floor. He looked on the workbench and saw tools scattered all over the place and started remembering where they all went and what for.

That was when another vision overtook him. This time, he saw the moon … our moon. The flag was on it. Then he was looking toward earth from the moon, and it was starting to get closer. Closer, closer, until he was orbiting the planet. Then into the planet. It got bigger, bigger, bigger, until he was looking at his house. Then through the garage roof, until he heard, "George!" There was a loud voice in his head and a figure in a robe in front of him. From the voice, it sounded female. She took her finger and stuck it sideways into her mouth. She started moving it fast up and down. "George, I am your sister!" She pulled the hood down while chuckling. "God, I love that bit!"

CHAPTER 8

Family?

"BUT I REALLY am your sister, George." She took off the robe to reveal a woman dressed as a scientist. "We've been monitoring your planet for many years, looking for you, and then during Shark Tank, which is one of my favorite shows by the way, there you were, plain as day, my little baby brother! So, you must have some questions … so … go!"

George walked over to her and waved his hand right through her. "How are you here?"

She quickly responded, "Ahh … the obvious first question. I just lost a bet. But okay, you could've asked about our parents or even my name. My name had the most on it."

George bursts in, "Hello!"

"Okay, okay!" she chimes back. "I, too, am an inventor on our planet, and this little baby is one of mine when I was eleven years old and you were … um, eight, I think. It's called a cranial projector, and I can travel through galaxies with it without fear of hitting anything or burning up in the suns, freezing in deep space, you know, stuff like that. We tried using it on you for most of your life, but we could only get a few moments. I think the longest we got was five minutes. So, I'm really on my planet talking through your brain because we need you, George."

He interrupted, "Let me guess, your planet is dying because you used all of its natural resources and now you need a new one to migrate to. And you were named after a star like Orion or something, and I'm just plain George."

She does an awkward smirk like he's way off. "No, my name is Beth and why does everyone always think the planet's dying and it's the end of everything? That's not a very good outlook. It's your planet that needs help. And I didn't name you, our parents did, and they are extremely dysfunctional!"

Now George was pacing back and forth, looking at the floor, occasionally looking up at his new-found sister. "Is your planet like ours, mountains, lakes, oceans, gravity, sun, moon, etc.?"

No hesitation. "Yes, we, too, have a sun and experience day and night."

He snapped back. "Is there different races?"

"Yes"

"Is there war, religion, politics?"

"Yes, yes, and yes, same problems, different worlds, different galaxies, are you just about finished?"

George stopped pacing, walked up to her, and said, "You seem pretty advanced. What do you want from me?"

"There it is!" she yelled. She raised her hands like she making goal posts and quickly brought them back before she's seen out of character. "The ultimate final question! Okay, for about a thousand years or so, there was this transport company that could get in and out of galaxies and planets without being seen using an advanced technology involving forward and reverse magnetism technology. Very few even knew of their existence because they used the oceans as a docking point. On most planets like ours, the oceans are so vast. They cannot explore the bottom, so it makes for the ultimate hiding place. About two years ago, their race died unexpectedly, and no one has been able to find them or their ships. But we know there is one on your planet in what you call the Bermuda Triangle. I can place a point above the ship in your head. All *you* have to do is figure out the technology, and get the ship to me so that we can begin intergalactic travel between our two worlds and finally meet face to face, where all your questions will be answered." She started to blink. "Uh-oh, powers fading … got to charge this damn thing … I'll be in—" She was gone.

CHAPTER 9

Invention

THIS WAS A lot to take in. How can he figure out technology he's never seen before? How can he get to the bottom of the ocean? He's an alien? Well, at least that makes sense. He'd always felt a little out of place anyway. But how did he get here from there? Surely, the advanced technology would have to compensate for Einstein's theory of relativity, or everyone would be old or dead by the time he had returned from another galaxy. Unless they found a way to travel so fast that time was irrelevant. Instead of planetary travel taking months like they do now, they found a way to travel through galaxies, and nothing so far has even tickled the power needed for that.

She said it was reverse magnetic technology. Did that mean by reversing the magnetic field, it created a faster power? *No,* he mused to himself, *the pull of the magnets can only be so fast. But the pull would be so fast the eye could not see it in order to work. I must create this for further study.*

And so he started. The side door to the garage opened slightly, but George is too involved to notice. It was Mr. Green. No doubt checking to see how his latest acquired project is working …

CHAPTER 10

Bada Boom

GEORGE SCRIBBLED DOWN a list of things that he needed, walked out to the car with the watchdog in it, and tapped on the window.

"Tell Mr. Green I need these things right away." The window rolled down, he tossed the list in and hurried back, slamming the door shut behind him. One billion was the deal Mr. Green had offered him. But that was before he'd met his sister. Now all deals were off. He knew he must tell him something to get to the bottom of the ocean, but he figured if he gave him his device, he would go away, and the money would pay for whatever he needed.

So he started on one magnetic wheel using a fan blade from a plastic ceiling fan for a bathroom. It has a metal axle between the blades attached to a little electrical motor. He thought to himself, *If I reverse the polarity of the motor to receive power, then the wire going to it will become live as if it was a generator, and it should be enough to shut up Mr. Green once he's powering a small lightbulb. Then his (or the government's) technicians will just enlarge it to power bigger things. The amount of spin will only generate so much spin unless I can find a way to make the spin faster. The metal axle will also be a problem because it affects the way the magnets chase each other, so I will have to fabricate it from graphite so there is no magnetic properties.* All of this he spoke in his own mind as if he is narrating the experiment.

His supplies arrived, and he stacked the snow blowers and lawnmowers on top of each other to make space for walking back and forth to various machines that he'll use for precision parts making, like a lathe, a band saw, a drill press, vice, dremel. After several hours of hit and miss, he finally got the magnetic wheel to spin. It started to make a whirring noise unlike anything he's heard before, and he admitted to himself that it was a little exciting. He lifted his glasses to wipe the sweat from the last four hours and when he put them back on, Mr. Green was directly in front of him. Startled him a little, which irritated him. He observed that he always seemed to get angry whenever that man was around, which was a complete turnaround from who he really was.

"Is that it?" Mr. Green asked, pointing to a spinning object on a small base with wires running from it which powered a small wattage lightbulb that was screwed into a grounded little makeshift stand.

"Yes, that's it. Is this where you kill me?"

A slight chuckle from Mr. Green. "No, George, I'm not going to kill the one person that just brought the world into the future, but you are confined to your house with guards all around it." Mr. Green grabbed the spinning object and proceeded to head toward the door.

George loudly asked, "What about my money?"

Mr. Green pulled out a card and placed it on the bench. "It's already in your account and several others. Call the man on this card and he will give you all the info you need. Why, you have plans?"

George smiled. "I'm thinking of doing a little fishing."

And just like that, Mr. Green was gone. George sat back down at the bench, his mind reeling with anticipation.

He pulled out the other three magnetic wheels he had hidden beneath the bench on the shelf. Again, he thinks to himself, *If I put one on the bottom spinning clockwise, reverse the second, and repeat clockwise on the top, I'll have the middle pushing the other two to a much faster speed.*

But what really happened was that the reverse started going so fast, it disappeared and was replaced by a bright light. The whirring noise became a *fffsssshhh* sound, and George felt a rush of potential energy coming from it.

He grabbed a plastic knife from the workbench and tried to stick it into the light to see if it would melt, and *boom!* It exploded, sending him through the garage window and onto the lawn outside! He could barely lift his head up enough to see his house and garage collapse in on itself. Car alarms were going off everywhere! Windows miles away were shattering! A ringing in his ears, and pain everywhere on his body! He looked up at the night sky and was comforted by the stars when a very disturbed-looking Mr. Green stood over him, and said, "Something you want to tell me, George?" Sirens grew louder in the distance.

"Ow! I'll never do that again!" In his mind, he was still trying to piece it together, but he thought it was because the two forward moving magnetic wheels were spinning the reverse so fast, it created a power of its own. When he'd introduced the foreign object to the mix, it created instability, which caused the explosion. What amazed him was the light that glowed from it. He must know more about this.

"George, I'm going to get us a ride to the emergency room, then we're going to get fixed up, and then I'm putting you in an empty warehouse so you can finish whatever that was."

George looked up at him. "With all due respect, Mr. Green, I kept my part of the bargain when I handed you the device."

As the ambulance pulled up, Mr. Green's eyes locked on George's and he said, "You've just become a bigger threat to national security, do you really think I'm letting you go?"

CHAPTER 11

The Price

AT NIGHTWOOD GENERAL Hospital, George sat in the curtained-off room, waiting to be served. Mr. Green was already being treated. *All access has its rewards,* he thought. In front of the entrance were two guards, leaving no doubt they were here for George.

"It's not what you think, George." What? Who? He pulled the curtain open to the bed next door and tried to see who it was, but her head was facing the floor. She lifted her head from crying, and he saw that it was Mrs. Lederman from next door. A silver-haired woman who was raising her granddaughter Emma on her own after a lengthy custody battle against her own son and abusive daughter-in-law after much neglect and drug use. They were in jail for another year. She used to come over for coffee every other day, or sometimes every day because he and Emma had become quite close.

"Sara, what's wrong? What's the matter? Is Emma all right?"

She continued sobbing. "Your invention ... people get hurt. I told her we don't need the leaf blower right yet, and you will tell me when it's ready, but she insisted."

He was no longer listening. His heart was racing! He rushed past the ER nurse to get to where she was. Tears were starting to well up in his eyes. He turned back to the nurse. He knew her. "Betty, tell me where Emma Lederman is."

She looked up from her desk and said, "She's in intensive care, George, you can't—"

"Betty!"

She could see his serious look. "I'll tell them you're coming."

He used to be here often with his wife and knew the staff on a first-name basis. After reaching the ICU, he went to each room, looking at charts, till he saw her name. Room 4.

The two guards had followed him there and stood outside. She was hooked up. Tubes in her mouth, IVs, a cast on her left leg, and one on her right arm. Burns on her face and hands. He was overcome with grief.

Maybe some of his grief was still left over from his wife, but he dropped to the floor on his knees, buried his head into his arms, and clasped his hands together. His hands brushed up against her as he cried. "I'm so sorry, God, please, let her live." He thought of all the times she'd come over to visit when Sara said it was okay after school if she did her chores and her homework, which she always did quickly. She was full of energy, always had a million questions about everything. She'd just started talking about boys and how Sara had just purchased her first training bra. She was just quirky enough to pull George out of the slump he was in since his wife died. He just couldn't stop sobbing. She was his only close friend. She must have sold him two hundred boxes of Girl Scout cookies that he had in his closet (he told her he ate them). He remembered adjusting the seat on her bike, fixing the flat, taking her to get ice cream at the local Dairy Queen. Babysitting her when Sara had to work.

When she was shopping, she always found safety in him. "God, I never ask of you … but this girl … I need her …" He felt her hand gently touch him, and he picked his head up from the blanket to see her eyes barely opening. "Tinker Man …" She always called him that. He could barely hear her with the tubes in her throat, so he leaned in and put his ear close to her mouth. "I saw it … I saw your light. It was awesome. And I know about the cookies …" She slipped back into unconsciousness. He just stood there, hoping she would come out of it but … nothing. He remembered (now that the shock was wearing off) she always came in through the doggy door he had when his wife was alive. He was going to board it up, or get a new door, but she was the only one who used it, and he saw no harm in it … till now.

Betty came into the room. "George, we have to examine you now. You'll be able to see her later. Also, you are a VIP, so we have a private room with a guard outside courtesy of Mr. Green. He knew how upset you are, so he thought you could get some rest in this room."

She led him to a room, after his exam, with couches, soft lights, a television, a little kitchenette, a coffee table, etc. It was the nurses' lounge. George put his legs up on the table; a heavy sigh escaped his lips. He stared off into space. The first dull moment in a while. Betty turned to tell him she'll be back, but he was already out. Slightly snoring. She shut the lights. Smiled at the guard and quietly pulled the door shut.

CHAPTER 12

Mr. Green Revealed

ELSEWHERE IN THE hospital, in a conference room that was commandeered, a private meeting was about to get underway. At the head of this meeting was Mr. Green.

"Gentlemen, you all know why you're here. The billion dollars you've invested is paying off tenfold. Even now, the magnetic engine is being built on a larger scale with all the different applications being considered for the future. What you don't know is our mutual friend, Tinker, accidentally discovered something never before seen that, if harnessed, could be weaponized in an unstable nuclear environment." He surveyed the table. Various aged men were seated at a twenty-four-foot table, all nodding in agreement, when one spoke up. "What have you done to secure such a weapon?"

A smile crossed his face. "He has kids, two sons. Steps are being taken even as we speak to ensure he cooperates enthusiastically. And since then, I've discovered his affection toward a little girl. She's here in this hospital. A neighbor's kid that he's fond of. That's all I have to say."

An older man on his right said "You know we're crossing lines here, lines we can't come back from."

CHAPTER 13

It's on Now

*H*E'S DREAMING . . . *he knows he's dreaming. He's traveling through space in an unknown ship. And yet, he knows how it works. He reaches an unknown planet, and the ship automatically heads for the ocean. But, wait, he can stop it. Just above the water, it hovers. He waits . . . somewhere in the distance, it's a ship . . . closer, closer . . . it's his sister, Beth. She's waving from the helm . . . now he sees her speaking.*

"George! George! George!" He slipped back to consciousness and someone shaking him.

"George! Wake up!" a man is in front of him with a familiar voice. "W- who ... who are you?" Everything was foggy, and he slipped on his glasses that had fallen during his sleep. Now he saw it was the soldier from the helicopter.

"Oh hey! I remember you, they had no idea who you were at the base in—"

"Not now, George! I'll explain later, Right now, you are in danger!"

The soldier pulled him up, walked him to the door, and cracked it open ever so slowly. A fellow soldier nodded back. He flung the door open, and they rush out into the hallway, where they see the unconscious guard being dragged and stuffed into a closet. George also noticed the cameras have been shot out in the lobby. The nurse, Betty, had been knocked out cold in her isolation booth. They reach a waiting ambulance outside, and George saw Emma in a gurney.

"What's going on here? She needs medical treatment! Please do not hurt her."

The soldier looked at him. "We're saving her, George. Mr. Green is plotting against you. He is not what you think. He intends to use her as a means to destroy you after you build his weapon."

This is most likely true, George thinks to himself. He seriously can't stand that guy.

There were two soldiers up front, one talking to George, one watching out the back window. All were wearing black and masks, so you can't see their faces, except for one that was talking to George. He looks like he was chiseled out of a Greek God magazine with movie star looks, sparkling blue eyes, and blond hair tucked up under the black stocking hat he was wearing. His very voice had a calming effect and a good nature about it.

"Where's the other one?" George asked. He remembered there were five of them.

"He's behind us in that black Camaro to create a road block if need be."

George peeked out the window. "Who the fuck are you guys?" He was desperate to understand all this.

"It's like you said, George, man cannot fathom God."

"So you are God?"

"No! You might know me as Gabriel."

George was startled. "Gabriel? But you were only mentioned in the Bible about … um … two thousand years ago?"

Gabriel smiled. "Why is it always about time with you earth dwellers? God does not have time, God is time. In your short life, you cannot understand. It's not meant for you to. Did you ever feel like you were lost inside someone else's dream?"

George shook a confirmation nod. "That's because you are. What you call reality is his proving ground for souls. And you, George, have one that he's looking for."

George was skeptical, to say the least. "Why doesn't he just kill me and take it?" A fair question for sure.

"It's your will, your mind, your essence, all culminating together that chooses to serve him for the benefit of mankind. Our world and your sister's world are very similar in their stages of existence. He believes your travel and invention will unite the two worlds and stop the end times for a while. For there is nothing like a common enemy to unite people. He has chosen you, George Tinker. Just like he did Noah, Moses, Isaac, etc., etc."

George was filled with questions. "What about Jesus? I thought he was the last. George had really learned something from those Sundays at the Nightwood Church.

"Jesus returns with an army, that's true. I will be there. After the seals are broken, there's no turning back. But they have not been broken yet, George."

Just then, gunfire erupted from outside. The one called Gabriel looked out the back window. George pushed over next to him and saw the Camaro shooting back at several black SUVs that had taken both lanes of the highway and were trying to pass. Then several more just seemed to appear from nowhere. George was starting to get nervous for the first time since this all began. A squelching noise on Gabriel's walkie-talkie. "Gabe … I'll see you soon …"

Gabriel responded, "Okay, my brother." And the Camaro turned sideways and started to roll and flip!

George yelled, "Ohhh!" And then there was something he's never seen before. A translucent angel with a fifteen-foot wingspan lifted slowly from the car. He raised a sword he held in his hand and created a wall of flame, which caught all the SUVs on fire and lit up the night sky. He then shoots off into the night sky, toward space.

George's jaw was wide open in amazement. His eyes were bugging out of his head! He looked back and calmly walking through the flames without even so much as a scratch was Mr. Green. He looked right at George's glowing face in the window, pulling farther and farther away to put fear into him.

"Did you see that?" George was feeling very small. "What can I do against that?" He grabbed Gabriel's shoulder to shake him. Gabriel grabbed his in response. "Just calm down, George. It looks bad, I know, but you have help, and we will not let you fail." His touch calmed George, and it was back to business as usual.

"Where are we going?" Gabriel kept a steady eye out the window. "We're going to a hidden convent in the mountains of Vermont, where we will be safe. We've also picked up your two sons and their families to make sure, and then … we wait."

George had to know. "Wait for what?"

Gabriel smiled. "For your sister to send that map to your head."

CHAPTER 14

The Mountain

"GEORGE! GEORGE! HELLO!" He struggled to awaken. It was her, Beth, in his room … Beth! He jumped up.

"Takes a long time for this thing to charge, I'm working on improvements. So how have you been doing, George? I see you're still alive, so that's a plus."

He still was not used to her not being there, so he passed his hand through her again. "You wouldn't believe what I've been through."

She smiled in acknowledgement. "Yes, yes, I would, George. Strange things are happening here as well. Our country is run by an evil bitch, and I'm afraid for my life sometimes. Listen, George, I'd love to chat with you, I really would, but this thing runs out of power quickly, and we're dealing with some serious shit here. So let me put this map in your head and what we know of their language, and you must hurry, George, please!"

She faded while she appeared to be … crying? George started walking with his hands in the air on the invisible typewriter. He saw the edge of the land pulling away. Clouds above darkening, ships dials all spinning in a whirlwind of malfunction. Then the scene traveled underwater, down, down, until he saw strange symbols on a piece of metal sticking out of the coral reef. The symbols changed before his eyes to become words in his own language. LGM TRANSPORT COMPANY … then back to reality.

Gabriel was standing next to him. "George, you okay? You were heading for the window."

George looked out the window. It was a cool autumn night. They are on top of a mountain and the view was incredible. The moon was full and its shine seemed to envelop the whole valley and the other mountains around it.

"I know where it is." He knew he was gazing upon this view for the last time. "Why is it safe here?"

"You are on holy ground." Gabriel's eyes seem to pierce his soul. "I'm not going to withhold any more, George. You are in it. We were told your mind can handle the information so … here goes everything. God knew man would fail. The stain in his nature. The potential to do evil is the price of free will. All governments are corrupt. Anytime someone is smart enough to lead the people, they feel like they should be above them. Although there are a few exceptions, they usually end up dead by the reigning evil one like Mr. Green. Similar scenarios have been played out many times in many universes. Each universe has twelve planets that rotate toward the sun until the very last one is no longer in the right place to support life. Then the sun collapses in on itself, which creates a black hole as you would call it, but really … it is the end of what you conceive as time."

George was fascinated by this new revelation. But also scared. "So this means earth was not the first? Nor will it be the last. But this must take trillions of years before—"

He's stopped short. "Time does not exist for God. There are no limitations or restraints to stop him. He wants a family to love that chooses him, and when he does things, he does them in a big way. He is the ultimate spirit, existing forever. He chooses wisely who spends that time with him."

George thinks of his wife. "And what about death?" His promise.

"Don't worry, George, you'll see her again. Love is the most powerful bond between spirits, it even goes beyond death. The capacity for great love is why mankind still exists at all. It's the only thing worth saving, and it pleases God to see it and feel it from his greatest achievement, humans. He will wipe away your stain of evil if you have to love in such a way. But, alas, most give up on him. He must constantly keep proving himself. It's when he gives up on man … well … that's where we're almost at George. When you see us angels, his servants, it's a sign that either man changes or …"

George was nodding. "Yeah, yeah, I get the picture. Now what about Mr. Green?"

Gabriel looked out into the night as well. "Every planet has one. A bad angel. Thinks he has the power to rule. Usually starts out like us, next to God. Then becomes corrupt. They take as many lower angels with them as they can, and they become demons. And this creates the universal chess match which plays out time after time across numerous galaxies."

Without even batting an eyelash, George said, "Why me again?"

"It's your understanding of things, George, without anger. Mr. Green made you mad, we were watching, but that's what he does. It's anger that actually leads people away from love. Then they see themselves as evil and feel guilt, then they are no longer united. It's the division that Mr. Green hopes to achieve. Divide you from each other, divide you from God, divide the different races using anger and fear. And then you fail. We have destroyed many without question once they reach this point."

"But what about babies and children? Surely they have not sinned enough to call for death?" George always wondered this.

"Ahh … the blood of the innocent. They've got a free pass straight to God, not corrupted, pure, they are God's extra strength. They will be great allies in the upcoming battle at the end of time, between all the good and all the bad. For not just children, but the blood of all the innocent has to reach a certain point for the Creator of all things to want to destroy his creations. Our planet and your sister's planet are almost there, and time is of the utmost importance. We will fly a helicopter to a private airport where a Lear jet will fly us to Miami. From there, we have a ship to take us to your coordinates. And George … expect trouble."

CHAPTER 15

Good-Byes

ON HIS WAY out, George greeted his sons and their families. They both have newborn babies. His oldest, Joshua, had a daughter all dressed in pink with cuteness to spare. George touched her hand, and she grabbed his finger and won't let go.

She gave him a big toothless smile that warmed him to the core.

"Her name is Susan, Dad. And you remember my wife, Lauren."

He embraced her, then both of them. "You are a great joy to my heart." Then he headed toward Jason, his younger son, who held up his son. "Jason Junior, Dad."

George leaned in and kissed him on the cheek and noticed that he, too, is adorable. He looked over to Jason's wife. "Hello, Diane, how have you been?"

She embraced him with tears in her eyes. "You come back safe, George, we'll be praying for you."

She kissed his cheek like it was the last time. Then a final embrace with his sons, who say they love him again when Gabriel grabbed his shoulder and tugged him out of the room while he tried to fight back tears. They walked into a long dark corridor leading to the stairs out when faintly behind him, he heard, "Tinkerman?" He stopped dead in his tracks. He knew she was here, but he thought she was sedated. Somehow, she knew he was leaving. He felt his heart coming out of his chest as he heard her dragging her cast to get to the door.

Then she said it louder. "Tinkerman!"

He broke Gabriel's grip on him and started running toward her as she came around the corner of her room, trying to hold on to the wall and dragging her foot. She still had a bandage on her head. "Tinkermaaan!"

He reached her just as she was about to fall over and scooped her up into his arms to embrace her as tightly as possible without hurting her. "Don't go, don't go, pleeease don't go, Tinkerman!"

He felt her trembling like she was deathly afraid. "I've got to, Emma, but I promise I'll be back soon!"

"But I'll have no one if you don't come back. Pleeease, Tinkerman!" He lifted her head off his shoulder and put his forehead right to hers. "Look into my eyes. I swear to you I will return, and I will take care of you. In the meantime, my sons will take care of you. You need to help them with their babies until I return. Can you do that for me?"

She put her head on his shoulder and clenched even tighter like she wasn't letting go. That's when Gabriel touched her arm and she became calm instantly. She slipped out of the embrace and back down to the floor, where a nun had grabbed her to keep her from falling.

"Will you sign my cast, then, before you go?"

George looked at Gabriel with a dumbfounded look on his face. Gabriel just grinned. Once they were in the helicopter, he asked, "How did you do that?"

Gabriel smiled. "Finger of peace ... it's a gift from God. We've had to use it through time on soldiers in battle, occasional crying babies, mothers, etc."

George just smiled. "I was just going to say, you guys would be great babysitters."

Gabriel looked right at him and said, "We should be. We've been doing it for mankind since time began!" And the helicopter lifted off.

CHAPTER 16

The Chase

STAYING CLOSE TO the treetops, they tried to stay under the radar and away from the city lights. About a half mile from the private airport, the pilot yelled, "We're being pinged!"

Gabriel yelled out, "Get us close to the ground!" The helicopter dropped down to a small clearing as close as they can to the ground without stopping.

"Jump!" George started to shake a little as the grass got closer, so Gabriel gave him a little push.

"Bend your knees!" he heard as he went out. Even with the bent knees and rolling with the motion, it still hurt like hell, but he did it. Gabriel and two others landed with him, but the pilot aimed right for the source of the missile, which exploded the aircraft. About three seconds later, again, a giant wingspan on a translucent white angel slowly rose from the fiery crash. He opened his arms, only this one held a scepter. The men with the launcher were incinerated instantly.

"What now?" George knew the answer, just not the details.

Gabriel pointed. "Half a mile or so that way is the jet."

They started running toward the trees, and once inside the tree line, Gabriel pulled out a .45 caliber pistol, clicked the safety off, put it in George's hand, and said, "Just point and shoot, anyone but us."

George stuck it in his hand and kept running. They can see the chain-link fence of a small airport in the distance, and they quickened their pace. All were dressed the same way: all in black, with two wearing masks. George and Gabriel were without masks.

There were sounds of men running behind them, and flashlights criss- crossed through the woods as they reached the fence. Gabriel bent down and easily pulled the fence up high enough to let them through, then let it back down and scaled the fence easily. They all started running toward the jet as it taxied down the runway slowly with the stairs still out. Then George heard it. He didn't believe it, but when he turned around to look, sure enough … it was a dog! Not just any dog, but a big, mean, ugly, vicious-looking bull mastiff, gaining fast. George turned as the dog leaped and *bang!* They both fell. George jumped up and shoots three more shots into the already dying dog out of fear and nerves. Then he ran over and grabbed the stair rail to start climbing it. Once inside, Gabriel pulled the stairs in and the jet sped up and took off.

George was sweating his ass off while Gabriel was as dry as a bone. "Did you see that?" His eyes were still bulging from the rush.

"Yes, George, you used too many bullets, give me your gun." He handed it to Gabriel. Gabriel reached into his pocket, popped the clip out, filled it with bullets, then popped it back in. He handed it back. By the time they reached cruising level, they have already passed Boston and opted to fly along the East Coast shoreline—low and out of radar. So they dropped out of the sky to hug the ocean and managed to stay flying for three hours till they reached Florida's edge, when a pilot burst on to the radio. "This is the United States Air Force, and you are in a restricted flight path. You must land at once. Please respond."

The pilot aimed straight up, and two fighter pilots followed. Once high enough, they leveled off. Everyone started putting on parachutes, and Gabriel quickly slapped one on George.

"When I say, pull this one. If it doesn't work, pull this one."

George looked as the pilot yelled, "They've got a lock!"

George yelled out, "What if that one doesn't work?"

But it was too late. The emergency hatch popped open, out they went into the night sky. The fighter pilot radio's in, "Possible drug smugglers exited jet, could we get a Coast Guard cutter to pick them—is that an angel?"

All three jets exploded in midair! Falling … falling … Gabriel yelled, "Now!"

George pulled the ripcord; with a sudden jolt, he was floating toward the dark black ocean. No sky above, for this area was stormy. But at the moment, it was just a drizzle. He sees land not too far off in the distance.

The water gets bigger, bigger, bigger, *splash!* He's under, clawing his way to the surface and gasping for air. Gabriel swam up behind him and cut his chute free. "Can you swim?" George nodded yes, and they started toward shore. As the sand got within reach, they heard the Coast Guard cutter behind them.

A voice crackled out on the bullhorn. "Where are you going, George?"

It was Mr. Green. George's heart sank. He looked back at the ship in the blackness of night and saw for the first time that all of his followers' eyes were white like they were blind or soulless.

George and the three others hit the shore while men jumped onto motorized rafts from the ship. Gabriel looked at his fellow soldier on the right and nodded. "I got this one," he said and pulled his mask off. He enlarges to a giant winged angel who opened his arms like the others, only this one held a scroll as he floated skyward and everyone in the ocean ignited like a bonfire with gas thrown on it! Dune buggy engines roar in the distance, about a quarter of a mile down the sand. Gabriel yelled, "Run!" And the remaining three ran for the town lights in the distance. After a few minutes, Mr. Green could be heard yelling, "You're running out of angels, George!"

As the ship and the lifeboats burned in the distance, Mr. Green walked up to the approaching dune buggy and climbed in the passenger seat. Several buggies roared off in pursuit.

CHAPTER 17

Small Town Blues

"WE MUST HURRY, George!" Gabriel and the one remaining soldier were pulling ahead of him.

"Sorry, it's been a while since my last triathlon. How much farther do we have to go?" He was a little winded.

"We're one town away, we've got to get a vehicle." Gabriel surveyed the scenery and saw a pickup truck outside a little diner. They ran to the vehicle, and it was locked. A quick look inside the diner revealed the owner taking up most of the stool. Everyone ducked down.

"Can you splice the wires if I get us in, George?"

Before he even said yes, Gabriel had smashed the window and opened the door in front of George. He quickly reached under and pulled the ignition wires out. He bit them, pulled the casings off, and twisted them together. The engine cranked up. "Move over, George."

Gabriel jumped in the driver's seat as the other soldier jumped in the back. The big man from the diner heard it start up, and as quickly as possible, came out while pulling out a pistol from inside of his coat, pointing and shooting wildly. But he noticed there were six shots, and he only fired three. He turned around to see three dune buggies projecting onto the street from the beach while shooting.

He stood with a blank stare as they passed him by. The soldier in the back lay down in the truck bed and began firing as they hit the one road leading to the next town. The speedometer was reading seventy on the dash. At seventy, one big bump will lose his remaining soldier, so Gabriel yelled "Shoot!" to George.

George was not ready. "What?"

Gabriel said, "Aim for a tire, George."

George looked in the mirror real quick and thought, *Hmm … at 70 mph my bullet must ricochet off the asphalt at a 47 percent radius to hit the tire with enough velocity to pop the tire, which will cause a steering shift in the front end, making it lean forward toward the right side into immoveable objects.* He leaned out the window, looked directly at Mr. Green in the buggy behind the one he was aiming for and fired.

The buggy careened into a parked car and exploded. Mr. Green looked back at the buggy on fire, then looked at George, and with a truly astonished look on his face, yelled out, "How does this geeky inventor keep killing my demons? I had less trouble with Da Vinci!"

George shrugged his shoulders, gave him a smirk, then slipped back into the truck. Even Gabriel said, "That's a first for me, George."

Gabriel knew in fifteen minutes they'll all be at the dock in Miami where the ship was, and he signals the soldier in the back, who nodded like he knew it was coming. He stood up and yelled, "See you on the other side, Gabriel," and leaped toward both dune buggies, sending them flying into the air while exploding!

A giant angel lifted from the wreckage and opened his arms as he was rising, "No! No! No! Every survivor but Mr. Green from the buggies ignited into flames. Stop killing my fuckin' demons!" he yelled as he slowly lifted himself from the pavement.

By now they were at the dock, and a medium-sized exploration ship with a two-man sub on it was preparing to make way when the bullet-hole-ridden pickup showed up. They both jumped out and run toward it.

CHAPTER 18

All Aboard

ALL OF A sudden, George stopped dead in his tracks. He heard a faint sob from somewhere and started looking around. "Someone is crying."

Gabriel shook his head. "No, George, we don't have time for this." And through a slight dawn mist, he saw her on an adjacent dock near the edge. She was looking into the water. He ran toward her. "Miss? Miss, excuse me, are you all right?"

As he inched up to her, he could see from behind that she was beautiful. Long brown hair rested down past her shoulders. A backless, skin-tight black dress and mini skirt flattered her well-toned legs that had wrapped strands leading down to four-inch stilettos.

"It's just not worth it," was what he heard as she started to go over the edge. George grabbed her and scooped her up into his arms before she hit the dark, murky water. "Who … who are you?" As she turned her head to face him, he saw a remarkable resemblance to his deceased wife. His heart was beating like a tribute to King Kong! He also saw a mark on her face like she had just been hit. By tomorrow it will be a pretty good shiner.

"I'm George." As he held her in his arms, he forgot everything that has happened to him in the last week.

"G-G-George?" She stopped sobbing to look at him and when their eyes meet for the first time, George wondered how he could ever move another step without her.

"You're coming with me." And he ran toward Gabriel.

She said in a soft, sad voice, "Are you going to hurt me, George?"

He was now running up the gangplank. "Never."

CHAPTER 19

I'm Your Captain

MR. GREEN WALKED up to a nearby house and knocked on the door. His clothes were in perfect shape, but this time he had lost his cell phone. He was in rural Miami, about a half mile from the ocean, and the real estate was getting pretty fancy. He was at the house of a banker who came to the door with a shotgun and backed it open slowly. "Y'all comin' from the accident I heard earlier?"

Mr. Green looked at his half-asleep eyes and said, "You going to shoot me, Joe?"

A dumbfounded look came over his face. "Huh?" Suddenly, a sound like someone in his brain said, "Open the door," and he did. He lowered the shotgun.

Mr. Green then grabbed his arm, and his eyes turned white. After that, he set the shotgun down and walked into the kitchen, returning with his cell phone and his keys. He handed it to Mr. Green then headed toward the garage.

Mr. Green put it to his ear without even dialing. Someone answered at the other end, and Mr. Green started speaking, "Admiral, you know who this is. I need a ship. A big fuckin' ship!"

Joe pulled up in a brand-new BMW and opened the passenger door. The two drive off, heading toward the ocean.

CHAPTER 20

Triangle

THERE WAS A glass-enclosed area inside the ship facing the bow, and George carried her in and set her down on a chair. He knelt down and looked her right in the mascara-rung eyes. "Are you okay, miss … miss … I don't even know your name."

She saw kindness in his eyes. "Reese, my name is Reese. Reese Thompson from Miami Beach! My so-called boyfriend did this," she pointed to her face. "This is the third time, and I swore I would rather die than live in his world another second! He treats his dog better!"

George took off his jacket and wrapped it around her. "I smelled coffee when we first came in, would you like some?"

She nodded yes. "You mean, like a date? Cuz I sure would like to get cleaned up first."

A man walked over to help her below after Gabriel signals him. It was a priest. George looked around and saw the whole crew were priests. "No more angels, Gabriel?"

Shaking his head no, Gabriel responded, "It's just you and me, George. I'm actually glad you have a friend because I am not going with you in the spaceship. This will be our last time together."

"What ship?" Reese was standing there, wearing a black hoodie, black sweatpants, and boots. All of which were too big for her. She was next to a priest, holding a tray with a pot of coffee, cups, etc. She has washed her mascara off and took her place back on the chair. The ship rocked its way through an increasingly turbulent sea, for the storm had grown its velocity and fury. Suddenly, the control panel started going haywire on the ship. All the instruments were spinning!

"What does that mean?" George said as he points to it. Gabriel looked around the room to all involved and said, "That means we're here."

CHAPTER 21

Into the Drink

FROM A STORMY, choppy sea where they were barely able to see beyond the giant waves, with thunder and lightning overhead, to a sudden drop into calm, barely moving water. Like being in the eye of a hurricane, where the sky was cloudy, but there was no rain or lightning. It looked like a giant peaceful circle in the middle of the storm.

George went out to the bow and looked through the sunken ships until he saw it. A blue-and-white flag flapped below the waves, just like the vision from his sister. He yelled out, "It's right here!" He waved and pointed like a madman. The ship stopped as big anchors hit the water. Many men scrambled to lower the sub to a level they can climb in.

George tried to explain to Reese they are going to a spaceship underwater to get it to fly into space before this evil man killed him. He gave her the option to go with him, but told her she has almost no time left to decide.

The sub was lowered into the water. "You must hurry, George, Lucif—um, Mr. Green will not be far behind."

George knew this already. He climbed into the two-man sub and got a quick once-over with the controls. As the hatch was about to be shut, he took one last look at Reese, and thought to himself, "God, she's beautiful."

And then for a brief second, their eyes meet again. She yelled, "Wait!" She ran to the edge of the ship and climbed down to the sub. George shut his eyes and whispered "Thank you," as she got in behind him.

"I was dead anyway, George … till you saved me. Now you're stuck with me!" From the distance, a loud gun burst, a whistling noise, then the sea exploded near the ship with a giant plume of water raining down on everyone. Then another, even closer! It was Mr. Green in a destroyer, just entering the circle. He was holding on to the rail on the bow with both hands, laughing maniacally, and grinning with bloodlust because he knew he was about to finish this. Gabriel was dressed in a wetsuit and was testing his microphone. "George, can you hear me? Push the orange button to reply."

George answered back. "Yes!" An even closer explosion! "Dive, George, dive!" George pushed some buttons, pulled a lever down, and down below the surface they disappeared to the depths. Gabriel jumped in after them. Meanwhile, Mr. Green was on the ship, yelling, "Can't you hit a fucking thing? Sink that ship now!"

Two shells shoot out and whistle down to the backside of the ship as priests shooting back try to scramble. Direct hit. Completely blew apart the backside of the ship that brought them. As it started to sink, the remaining priests started to return fire with machine guns toward the fast-approaching vessel. Two more screaming shells destroy any and all remaining. Mr. Green's glowing red eyes could be seen, and his demonic laughter could be heard by the last of the dying priests. But, suddenly, he stopped. No angel was flying up.

"What are you up to, Gabriel?" he says to himself. He studied the water for a moment, then yelled, "Depth charges!"

A chill came over him like he'd been outsmarted. He'd felt it numerous times before. Depth charges started exploding underwater, sending the giant plumes of water into the sky. Down below, Reese was screaming every time one went off. George hit the orange button again. "Gabriel, we're here, I can see the ship's nose sticking out of the coral reef at the bottom, but how do I get in? We don't have wetsuits."

Gabriel descended to where they were. "I still have a few tricks left, George. I'll see you again one day, my friend and Godspeed."

Gabriel burst out of the mask and suit. Once he was in angel form, he was larger than all the others. He opened his arms and was holding something in his hand. The water from the alien craft and the sub became a giant bubble of air, and the sub hit the bottom with a giant thud! George popped open the hatch and yelled, "Hurry!" to Reese, who was still slightly in shock from all that had just transpired. He helped her out and they both run toward the craft.

George frantically started cleaning off debris till he saw what should be the door. Only he can read the inscription because of his sister. He found a hand imprint near a word that resembled enter and put his hand in it. The door slid straight up with a hissing noise.

Once inside, everything lit up, and they headed straight for the seats as the door hissed shut behind them. It was a saucer-shaped craft with two lines in the middle that split it into thirds. He can't see out. But he was starting to understand the control panel. He saw three switches next to a blue button. He hit the top switch and the top started spinning. A screen popped up and showed the top part. He hit the middle switch and the middle spun in reverse. It's just like his invention. After all three switches were engaged, the wall became translucent, and they can see out. The water filled in the bubble as Gabriel let it go. He pushed a little star button, and they shoot off with no G- force effect. In the meantime, Gabriel flew to the opposite side of the destroyer and stayed suspended for Mr. Green to see him. He walked to that side and said, "Gabriel, why are you here? Is our friend George dead?"

Gabriel looked at him like they've been dealing with each other for a long time. "We both know it's not your time to be put down, Lucifer … or Mr. Green, if you prefer. But you know it's coming, and we will be ready for your army when it's time."

A great bright light omitted from Gabriel, temporarily blinding everyone on the ship, except Mr. Green. Then he shot up toward the heavens.

Mr. Green had a feeling he was being stalled and turned around to see a saucer-like craft shoot out of the sea toward the sky at a high rate of speed. "Shoot that fuckin' thing down!" he yelled while pointing.

One of the possessed yelled back, "It's out of range of the guns!"

Mr. Green grabbed him and threw him to the ground. "Then nuke it!"

Five seconds later, a missile shot out and turned toward the direction of the craft. On George's screen, a red warning went off, and it showed the missile heading toward it. It was gaining ground as they reach the atmosphere. George was looking for flares or something to throw it off, when he saw a button blinking on the panel that looked like a wormhole, so he hit it. The middle started spinning so fast on the outside, and just as they were about to get hit with the nuke, they disappeared with a stream of light. The nuke just drifted toward deep space. George knew he was headed toward an unknown fate. But he also started to remember all that had happened. All who had died. He started to weep.

Rather than show his weakness in front of Reese, he turned away and looked down at the floor. Just then, a foot came into the area where he was looking. Then another. Then black sweatpants hit the floor in front of him. Then a black hoodie. He looked up and smiled …

Don't forget the exciting conclusion in the next title, *Tinkerman Too The Traveler.*

www.ingramcontent.com/pod-product-compliance
Ingram Content Group UK Ltd.
Pitfield, Milton Keynes, MK11 3LW, UK
UKHW022219230426
12048UKWH00016BA/941